D1362151

First published in 1989 by
André Deutsch Limited
105-106 Great Russell Street, London WC1B 3LJ

ISBN 0 233 98325 2

Printed by
Proost International Book Production, Belgium

JASON
AND THE
GOLDEN FLEECE

Francis Mosley

ANDRE DEUTSCH

There was once an ambitious villain, Pelias, who lived in Ancient Greece. He seized power from the King, his own brother. The brother had a son, Jason, who badly wanted the crown that was his by rights.

"I mean to wear my father's crown," he said to Pelias.

Pelias was frightened, but he was also cunning.

"You shall have it," he said. "But first you must bring me the Golden Fleece, in order that good fortune may return to our land."

The Golden Fleece, as Pelias well knew, hung from a tree in the land of Colchis, hundreds of miles away, across stormy seas. He also guessed, rightly, that Jason would not be able to resist the challenge.

Jason went to find Argos, the finest shipbuilder in all Greece, and asked him to build the sturdiest, fastest ship possible. Then he set out to find a crew. Among those he finally chose were Hercules, the strongest man in the world, and Orpheus, who could charm the birds from the trees with the music he played on his lyre. When all was ready Jason and his crew named their ship Argo and set sail. No one cheered louder than King Pelias as they left the harbour.

"That's the end of him," he thought cheerfully.

They rowed for three weeks across the blue Aegean sea until they came across their first obstacle, a narrow channel between two towering rocks. Wrecked ships lay all around.

"See those wrecks?" said Jason. "The rocks surge together whenever anything approaches. No one has ever got through alive."

His crew, brave though they were, did not relish being crushed to death. But Jason was clever as well as brave. He had a plan. He waited patiently until a pigeon flew past them, heading for the channel. At once the rocks clashed together and the pigeon only just managed to squeeze through, scattering a few broken feathers.

"Now!" yelled Jason, as the rocks moved apart again.

The Argo shot through before
they had time to crush it.

For weeks they rowed on; across stormy seas, past rugged
islands and gloomy coastlines till at last the mountains of
Colchis loomed ahead. The weary crew gave a cheer, the
ship was beached in a sandy cove and Jason leapt ashore.

"Stay here and guard the ship," he said. "I will go alone
to the King and ask him for the fleece."

After a journey of several days, Jason arrived at the King's castle. To his great relief the King welcomed him warmly, told him to rest after his long climb and ordered food and fresh clothes to be sent to his room.

"This will be easy," Jason thought to himself. "He seems friendly enough."

But it wasn't easy. "The fleece is yours for the taking," said the King with an unpleasant smile. "But it is the custom here to set a task before granting a favour. You have asked for a big favour, so you will have to perform two tasks. First, you must yoke two fire-breathing bulls to a plough and then plough a field with it. Second, you must sow a set of serpent's teeth in the freshly ploughed field."

"Serpent's teeth?" thought Jason. "What will they grow into? There must be a trick in this."

Brave as he was, Jason was worried. Even he didn't like the idea of facing fire-breathing bulls.

Fortunately for Jason the King had a daughter, called
Medea, who was famous for her skill in witchcraft. She
took a fancy to Jason as soon as she set eyes on him.

"I'll help you tame those bulls if you like," she offered.
"But you'll have to promise to marry me if I do."

"I was going to ask you, anyway," said Jason hastily.
"I'm looking for a bride, as a matter of fact, and you'll do
very well."

Pleased with the way things were going, Medea went off
to her workshop and prepared a magic lotion.

When all was ready for the first test Medea went with Jason to the field.

"Did you cover yourself with my lotion?" she asked him.

"Yes," he replied, "all over."

"Good." Medea smiled at him. "Put this stone in your pocket," she went on, "you may need it after you've sown the serpent's teeth."

The dreadful bulls were unleashed and charged at Jason, fire streaming from their nostrils. But Medea's lotion worked and the flames did him no harm. The bulls, knowing they had met their match, lowered their heads meekly and allowed Jason to place the yoke on their necks.

"Get up, there," he called and the ploughing began.

Back and forth went the bulls until the work was finished and the newly-ploughed earth glistened in the sunshine.

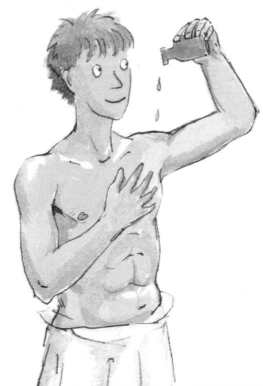

"So far, so good," said Jason cheerfully.

But the King, disappointed that his bulls had not made cinders of Jason, came forward carrying a bag filled with the teeth. Jason attached it to his waist and walked carefully across the field, scattering the teeth as he went.

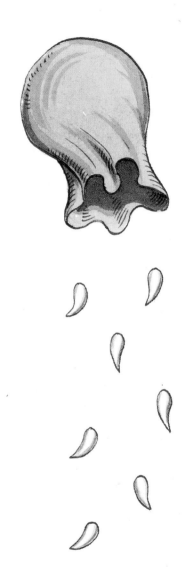

No sooner had the last tooth struck the ground than an
army of soldiers sprang up. They rushed towards Jason,
prepared to cut him down.

Jason put his hand in his pocket, grasped the stone and
hurled it at the nearest soldier.

   "I hope that's what Medea meant me to do with it," he
thought desperately.

   It was. The moment the stone struck the soldier he
turned on the man nearest him. In seconds the soldiers had
forgotten Jason and were fighting one another. Before
long not one was left alive.

Well pleased with himself, Jason went back to the palace.

"I've done what you wanted," he told the King. "May I have the Golden Fleece now, please?"

The King frowned angrily. "No, you can't," he growled. "I'm not giving it to you, you'll have to find it for yourself."

Once again, Medea came to the rescue. She led Jason to a tree in a forest where the Golden Fleece hung, guarded by a ferocious dragon.

"This dragon never sleeps," said Medea, "but if I can make friends with it, we'll see . . ."

She called softly to the dragon, as if it were a dearly-loved pet. The huge creature turned its head towards her and she tickled it gently under the chin, making it look up at her. As it did, she dropped a sleeping potion into its eyes.

"Sleep well, dragon," she whispered.

Jason leapt lightly over the sleeping dragon, snatched the fleece and ran down the hillside, followed by Medea.

Three days later they reached the sandy cove where the Argo and its crew were waiting for them. The ship was launched at once and, with their precious prize, they sailed away from Colchis for ever.

Jason, Medea and the Argonauts had one more adventure before they reached home, and this time it was Orpheus who saved them. One evening, at sunset, they heard the sound of distant but beautiful music. It was the Sirens, heartless mermaids of great beauty, singing the song with which they liked to lure sailors to their deaths on treacherous rocks. Unable to resist, the Argonauts rowed even harder. Then Orpheus taking up his lyre, played a tune with a melody even more entrancing than the song of the Sirens.

With his music in their ears, they rowed steadily on to safety.
A few weeks later they were home. Jason's uncle was not
among the crowd who came to welcome them. In fact, the
moment he heard of Jason's return, he fled the country.

Jason was crowned King and Medea, whom he married, became Queen.

All was not happy ever after, but that's another story.